THE MAGIC TREE

a tale from the Congo

adapted and illustrated
by Gerald McDermott

Henry Holt and Company ◆ New York

This is a tale from the Bakongo tribe of the Congo River basin in Africa. In graphic style, *The Magic Tree* is a reflection of the austere, stylized, low-relief carvings of Central Africa.

Henry Holt and Company, Inc.
Publishers since 1866
115 West 18th Street
New York, New York 10011

Henry Holt is a registered
trademark of Henry Holt and Company, Inc.
Copyright © 1973 by Landmark Productions Incorporated
All rights reserved.
Published in Canada by Fitzhenry & Whiteside Ltd.,
195 Allstate Parkway, Markham, Ontario L3R 4T8.

Library of Congress Cataloging-in-Publication Data
McDermott, Gerald.
The magic tree: a tale from the Congo / [adapted and illustrated]
by Gerald McDermott.
Summary: Retells a Congolese tale in which an ugly and unloved
twin discovers a magic tree that gives him everything he wants.
[1. Folklore—Zaire.]   I. Title.
PZ8.1.M159Mag   1993   398.2'096751—dc20   [E]   93-35588

ISBN 0-8050-3080-8

First Revised Edition—1994
Printed in the United States of America
on acid-free paper. ∞

10 9 8 7 6 5 4 3 2 1

Congo
River

Time was,
there lived two brothers,
Luemba and Mavungu.

Born as twins,
they grew
and came to be
very different.

Their mother loved Luemba.
She smiled on him always.
She gave him fruit.

Mavungu was
given nothing.

One night he left his home.

Mavungu came to a place in the river.
A great tree was there,
so thick he could not pass.

When he pulled
the leaves
strange voices
spoke to him.

Mavungu was astonished.

From each leaf,
a new person.

Last to come
was a beautiful girl,
a princess.

She thanked Mavungu
for releasing her people
from The Magic Tree.
She vowed that
she would care for him.

She touched a charm
around her neck.
"I want to be his wife,
but he is so homely."
Again she touched the charm.
"I want to be his wife,
but he is in rags."

Mavungu was joyful now,
joyful and strong.

After a time, they passed near a wide place by the river.
The princess made a magnificent village grow up there.

Mavungu married the princess.
They exchanged vows of love.
But she pledged him to silence:
   The source of his wealth and pleasure must always be hidden.
   The secret of The Magic Tree must never be told.

The sun crossed the sky many times.
The moon grew to fullness.
And Mavungu thought of his family.

He sent for his mother
and his brother.
When they came,
he treated them kindly.

But his mother
wanted to know
Mavungu's secret.

He began to tell
of his journey down the river.
The princess stared at him.
His words became as silence.

The sun crossed the sky
many times again.
Once more
the moon grew to fullness.
Mavungu could not forget
his family.

Alone, he returned to his mother's home.

"Mavungu,"
said his mother.
"You left me long ago.
Tell me of your new life."

Mavungu forgot
his pledge of silence.
He forgot
those who loved him.
And he gave his secret to those
who did not love him at all.

"I wed
the princess
of The Magic Tree
and she made
a magnificent
village.

"I have been
very happy
there.

"Oh!"

ABOUT THE AUTHOR

Caldecott Medalist Gerald McDermott's illustrated books and animated films have brought him international recognition. He is highly regarded for his culturally diverse works inspired by traditional African and Japanese folktales, hero tales of the Pueblos, and the archetypal mythology of Egypt, Greece, and Rome. It was his fascination with the imagery of African folklore that led him to the stories of *Anansi the Spider, The Magic Tree,* and *Zomo the Rabbit.*

Gerald McDermott was born in Detroit, Michigan. He attended Cass Technical High School, where he was awarded a National Scholastic Scholarship to Pratt Institute. Once in New York, he began to produce and direct a series of animated films on mythology in consultation with renowned mythologist Joseph Campbell. These films became the basis for Mr. McDermott's first picture books. Among McDermott's many honors and awards are the Caldecott Medal for *Arrow to the Sun,* a Pueblo myth, and a Caldecott Honor for *Anansi the Spider: A Tale from the Ashanti.* In addition, Mr. McDermott is Primary Education Program Director for the Joseph Campbell Foundation.